The Teddy Bear

For Noella, Martha, and Sam—

I'll be there soon.

Henry Holt and Company, LLC
Publishers since 1866
115 West 18th Street
New York, New York 10011

Henry Holt is a registered trademark of Henry Holt and Company, LLC
Distributed in Canada by H. B. Fenn and Company Ltd.

Library of Congress Cataloging-in-Publication Data
McPhail, David M.
The teddy bear / David McPhail.
Summary: A teddy bear, lost by the little boy who loves him, still feels
loved after being rescued by a homeless man.
[1. Teddy bears—Fiction. 2. Lost and found possessions—Fiction.
3. Homeless persons—Fiction. 4. Love—Fiction.] I. Title.
PZ7.M2427 Te 2002 [E]—dc21 2001001500

ISBN 0-8050-6414-1 / First Edition—2002 / Designed by Martha Rago
The artist used watercolor and ink on illustration board
to create the illustrations for this book.
Printed in the United States of America on acid-free paper. ∞
10 9 8 7 6 5 4 3

The teddy bear got to go places, too. He went
on trips—short trips, long trips. The boy
who loved him took him everywhere.

The teddy bear had a good home, a warm and cozy place to sleep, many friends, and someone who loved him.

The Teddy Bear

written and illustrated by

David McPhail

Henry Holt and Company • New York

One day, while traveling, the boy and his family
stopped for lunch.

In a moment of confusion
and forgetfulness . . .

. . . the teddy bear was
left behind.

By the time he was missed, and a search begun, it was too late—he was not to be found.

The teddy bear was unhappy and afraid. He lay squashed in a dark, smelly place, and even though he had a fine fur coat he was beginning to get a chill.

Long hours passed. The teddy bear was despairing of ever being found. Suddenly he felt fingers close around his leg and pull him free.

"Saved!" the teddy bear rejoiced. "My little boy has rescued me!"

But the hands that held him did not belong to the little boy. When his eyes adjusted to the brightness, the teddy bear saw that he was in the grasp of a bearded man wearing a long green coat. The man held up the teddy bear and stared.

Slowly, a smile spread across the man's face. Then he stuffed the teddy bear in his pocket and started walking.

The teddy bear spent the rest of that day in the bearded man's pocket as he ambled through the city streets.

Night came on, and the man made his way home. The teddy
bear lay awake looking at the stars as the bearded man slept.

That night, for the first time since the teddy bear
came into his life, the little boy went to bed without him.

In the morning the sad little boy went off to school . . .

. . . and the sad little teddy bear went back into the pocket of the long green coat as the man set out on his daily rounds.

Days passed.

Weeks went by, then months.

The boy still missed his teddy bear, but with each passing day, he thought about him less and less.

He had new toys to occupy him and new friends to keep him busy.

As for the bear, he missed the little boy and his old
friends. But he was enjoying his new life and the company
of the bearded man.

Best of all, the bear still felt loved.

The winter came to an end. The days grew warmer. The bearded man put away his long green coat.

Now he carried the bear under his arm as he went about his business.

One spring day the man placed the teddy bear on a park bench while he looked for something.

Now it just so happened that the little boy was walking
through the park that day with his mother and father.

As he was passing the park bench, the little boy
noticed the teddy bear.

"My bear!" he cried, scooping up his old friend in his arms and squeezing him tight.

"Amazing!" said the little boy's mother.

"How could this be?" said the little boy's father.

Then they saw the bearded man approaching.

"Come along," said the father.

"Mustn't be late," said the mother.

And they all walked quickly toward the park exit.

They were on the curb, waiting for the light to change, when they heard someone wailing.

It was the bearded man.

Standing in front of the bench, he cried out, "My bear! My bear! Where is my bear?"

The traffic light turned green. The sign blinked WALK.
But instead of crossing the street, the little boy ran back into
the park. Back to the bench and the bearded man.

"Is . . . is this your bear?" the little boy asked, holding the teddy bear out to the man.

The bearded man smiled.

He took the teddy bear in his rough hands and hugged him.

"Thank you," he said to the little boy. "I don't know what I'd do without him."

"I know what you mean," said the little boy. "I used to have one just like him."

Then, with his mother and father beside him, he
walked back to the corner to wait for the light to change.

DATE DUE		